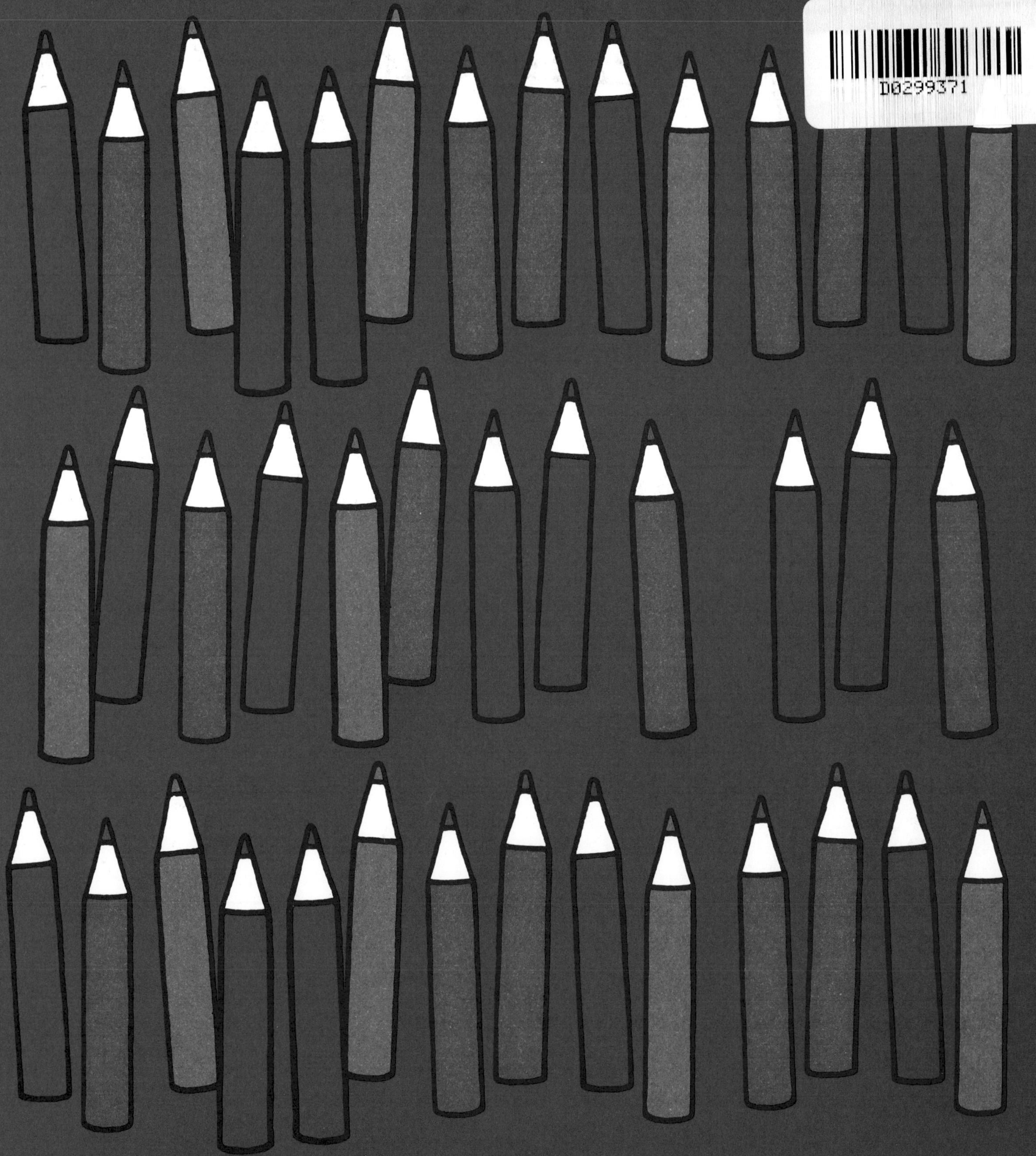

simon and schuster
First published in Great Britain in 2014 by Simon and Schuster UK Ltd
1st Floor, 222 Gray's Inn Road, London WC1X 8HB
A CBS Company
Publication Licensed by Mercis Publishing bv, Amsterdam
Illustrations Dick Bruna © copyright Mercis bv, 1953-2014
Design and text © 2014 Simon and Schuster UK

ISBN 978-1-4711-2283-5
Printed and bound in China
10 9 8 7 6 5 4 3 2 1
www.simonandschuster.co.uk
www.miffy.com

miffy's first day

SIMON AND SCHUSTER
London New York Sydney Toronto New Delhi

Today is Miffy's first day at school.

Miffy has picked out a new bag especially. Inside are Miffy's pencils and a packed lunch.

'Time to go!' says Mummy Bunny.

Find these stickers and add them to the picture:

The school is white with a red roof.

'We visited your school last week,' Mummy Bunny says. 'Do you still like it?'

Find these stickers and add them to the picture:

Miffy nods.

   'Hello, Miffy!' Miffy's new teacher says.

Suddenly, Miffy feels quite shy.

'We are going to have so much fun today!' says the teacher smiling.

Find these stickers and add them to the pictu

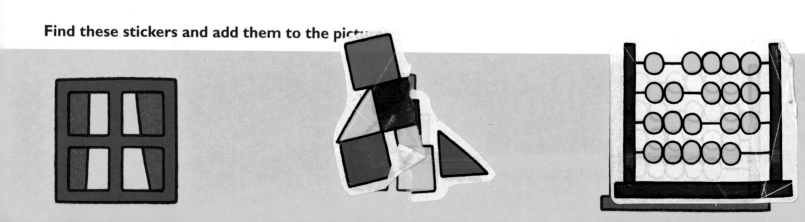

Mummy Bunny gives Miffy a big hug and a kiss.

'I will be here to pick you up at the end of the day,' says Mummy Bunny.

Then she waves goodbye.

Find these stickers and add them to the picture:

Miffy's teacher shows Miffy the classroom. There's a special place to put Miffy's coat and bag.

'Hello!' one of Miffy's classmates says. 'My name is Dan.'

Find these stickers and add them to the picture.

In the morning, Miffy's class plays indoors. There is a big cupboard of toys for everyone to share.

Miffy picks a train to play with.

Find these stickers and add them to the picture:

Next, Miffy's class play on instruments.

There's a trumpet, a xylophone and a drum. Miffy is playing the recorder!

Toot! Toot!

Find these stickers and add them to the picture:

 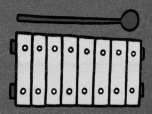 

At lunchtime, Miffy sits outside with her class.

All of this playing has made Miffy hungry! She eats the yummy lunch Mummy Bunny packed for her.

Find these stickers and add them to the picture:

Now it's time to play outside.

Miffy and her new friends have lots of fun playing in the sunshine.

Find these stickers and stick them on the picture:

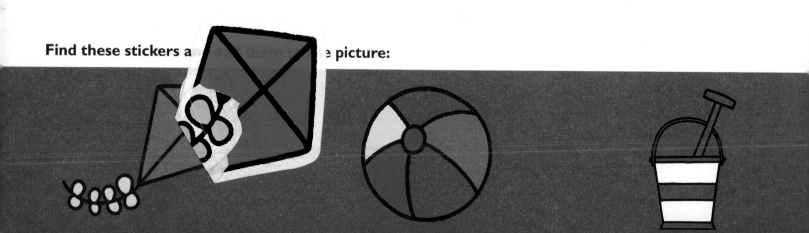

In the afternoon, it's time for art and craft.

Then everyone gathers round and Miffy's teacher reads a story.

Miffy loves story time!

Find these stickers and add them to the picture:

Miffy is having such a good time, she doesn't notice **Mummy Bunny** is here to pick her up.

The teacher waves goodbye to **Miffy** and her new friends.

Find these stickers and add them to the picture:

'Did you enjoy your first day of school?'
Mummy Bunny asks.
'Yes!' Miffy says. 'Can I go again tomorrow?'

Bye-bye!

Find these stickers and add them to the picture:

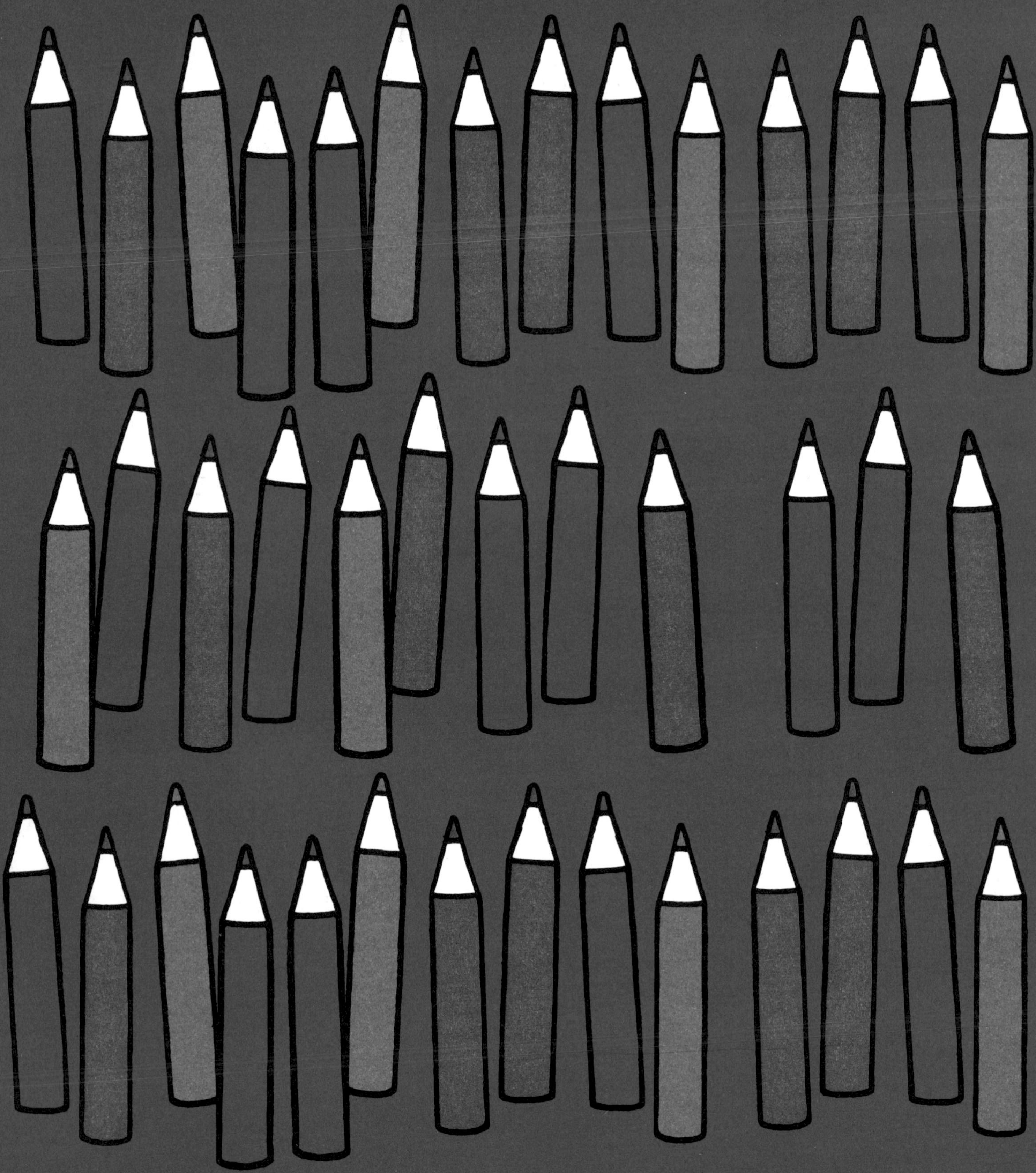

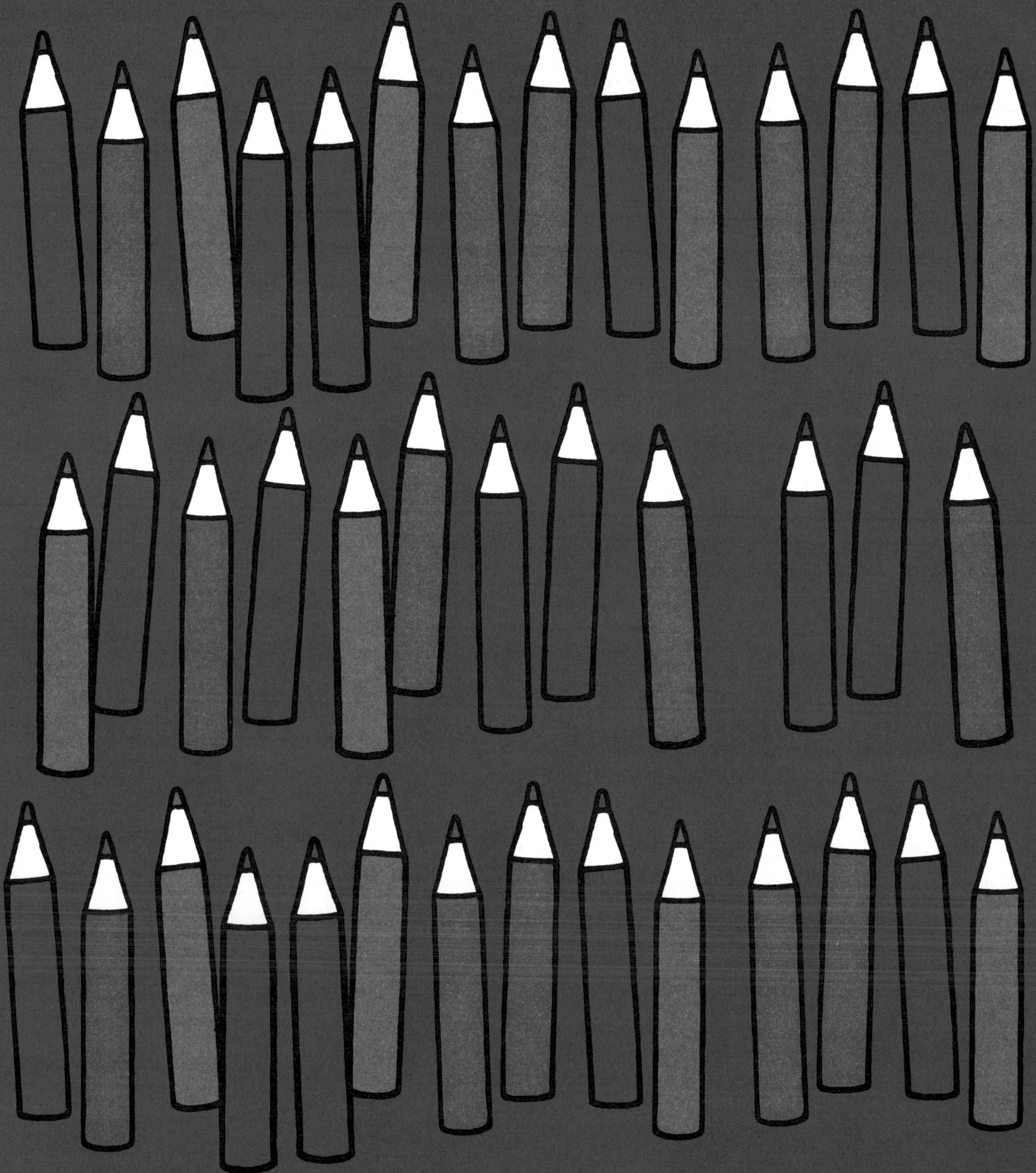